Gracie

by Carolyn Sloan

illustrated by Lisa Flather

LONGMAN

Chapter 1

There is a bright side to Carter's Market. Its people are cheery and busy. The stalls are warmly coloured — even the junk is polished here. The people who come to shop in the market often bring their dogs with them; brushed and combed, well-fed dogs on leads.

Gracie lives on the dark side of the market but she has never been brushed and hardly ever well-fed. Home is an arch in the deserted railway embankment, blackened with soot from the days when steam trains thundered overhead. The dark side smells of rot. People only go there to throw away their rubbish but the rubbish is never wasted. Every box and bone and cabbage leaf is eaten or used here. Mice and ants, spiders and worms all make homes in the stained cardboard boxes. There is a city of creatures to eat every last food scrap, and none of them grows fat.

Starlings and sparrows nest high up above the arches and rats have tunnelled into the crumbling stonework. Foxes often come at night, and an old lady comes at dusk with a paper parcel full of food for the wild cats. She shoos the dogs away.

"Why doesn't she bring anything for us?" Gracie once asked her friend, Taters.

"She's probably a witch," said Taters, whose mother told him scary stories. "Witches always like cats best." But they both waited that day, as usual, to see if the cats left anything. As usual, the cats gobbled up every bit of pie-crust and crumb of stale bread. "That's it, greedy, gobbling cats," said Taters. "Let's go and chase the rats around."

Gracie was young then, about half-grown, with paws that seemed to be several sizes too large for her. She was still a bit clumsy, but she was tough. She'd had to be in Carter's Market. Her mother was old, far too old to be having puppies, and too weak to care for them properly. She spent most of her days just lying on a piece of sacking in her arch. There was a time when Gracie had had two brothers, but they had made friends with some children in the market one day and the children had taken them home. When Gracie rushed to tell her mother, the old dog just sighed and said it was probably for the best, after all. Her mother had always told her that dogs who lived with people – home-dogs – weren't proper dogs at all; just softies who couldn't look after themselves. The only real dogs, she said, were tramp dogs, independent dogs, like herself. She was proud of being a tramp dog.

Gracie was shocked that her mother didn't mind about her latest sons becoming home-dogs.

"How can it be for the best?" she said, puzzled.

"I was too old to be a good mother to them," her mother said tiredly, "and they were always whining and wanting things. They weren't like you, Gracie. You can look after yourself, you'll always be all right because you're like me, girl. Those two, well, they'll probably like living in homes – being given their food, baskets with cushions to sleep on, little walks on leads and games in the park. I just hope they have good homes, that's all."

"You had homes sometimes," said Gracie, who liked hearing about them. "Did you never have a good home?"

Her mother sniffed in a rather rude way. "I had lodgings, dear, just occasionally, in very bad winters. That's not the same. I never trotted out on a lead or let people wash me, I can tell you!"

"Tell me more ... what were they like? How did you get to them?"

"There's a thing called Christmas," said her mother. "You'll find out. It's usually cold and damp and the market closes, and people sing a lot and buy holly and get jolly and start feeling sorry for people who aren't being jolly. It's a time when they feel sorry for dogs without homes and warmth and food ... You can easily get taken to a home at Christmas. "Oh poor doggie!" they say, "Let's give the little doggie to little Freddie for Christmas!"

"And?"

"And that's fine. Christmas lasts for about nine days, I think, and you get lots to eat and somewhere warm to sleep, and there are trees inside houses with lights on. I've known dogs who have chosen Christmas homes and stayed for ever and been happy ... not free like us, but ... well, okay."

"But you? You never did."

"I stayed somewhere once ... and when Christmas had gone, dear little Sweetie – that's what they called me – wasn't so sweet. It was 'that dog needs feeding, who's going to take it out ... wretched thing's chewed my boots, puddled on the floor again'. No, Gracie, homes aren't for dogs who want to be their own sort of dog. Know what I mean? Stay loose, girl."

"I don't want to stay here for ever."

"Don't. Move around, find somewhere else. Be a wanderer, that's the life. Don't stay here for long with that friend of yours, Taters, in the next arch. They're a villainous lot, that family. You don't need that much trouble."

"No," said Gracie, "it's fight, fight, fight. Snap, snarl, scrap, just for a place to sit down sometimes."

"You're a good pup, Gracie, soon you'll start to win. And winning's better than losing ... but keep moving on ... " She was exhausted. There was so much more that she wanted to tell Gracie ... be a wanderer ... be like me ... you're the best pup I ever had ... She fell asleep in the dirty sacking, and only her knobbly bones stuck out to show that she was there at all.

Gracie crawled out of the arch. It was time to scrap about and fight for food. She'd get some pickings ... she always did, although not the best. When she started to win fights, would that make any difference? She wasn't like Taters.

Taters was crouched around a greasy box of chicken bones and burnt chips, growling as if the chicken could still get up and fly away. When he had crunched all the bones and licked right into the corners of the box, he sat up and looked at Gracie.

"Why didn't you try and get it from me?"

"I don't like fighting. You know that – especially with you."

"You need the practice. I get lots of it. Know why? Because when I'm fully grown I'm going to be the toughest dog in the market. The Terror of Them All. I'll have a dog pack. You can join it if you like."

"No thanks," said Gracie, "I'm not going to stay here for ever." They sat, scratching in harmony, watching a poodle with a pale blue collar and a hilarious haircut tripping after a pair of high, clicketty heels.

"Look at that prissy pom-pom," snarled Taters rudely. "Let's chase it. Come on Gracie, I dare you … "

"Stupid," said Gracie, "It's against the rules, you know that. You want us all to be rounded up?"

Taters didn't. Rounding-up could be fatal. His mother had told him scary stories about that too, to make him obey the market rules. "Let's go and chase the cats then," he said, to take his mind off the poodle.

"No. I'm going to find some food for my mother now."

"Let her find her own food."

"She's sick. She's getting very old."

"Then she'll probably die," said Taters flatly. Gracie turned away, giving him such a hateful look that he was sorry.

"Well, she will," he said clumsily. "You've got to face it, Gracie, that's the way things are. You've got to be able to look after yourself."

Gracie refused to listen to him any more. But he was right. Her mother did die. And she did have to face it. Some other dogs moved into her arch and drove her away. Gracie knew she should have fought for her arch. She had been born there, her mother had died there. But now she didn't want it, she didn't want any more to do with the market. There had to be somewhere else, something better. Gracie shook herself, she stood proudly and looked round the market.

"Yes," she said firmly, "there's got to be a better life than this – and I'm going to go and look for it."

Chapter 2

Gracie left Carter's Market early one morning before the traders had come to set up their stalls. Only Taters was up, sniffing round for food or trouble.

"Maybe I'll see you again," he said, trying to pretend he wouldn't miss her, "and maybe I won't. Don't get run over. Cheers."

Gracie took the main road out of the town; it was quiet to begin with, the birds were just getting up and twittering to each other. Gracie was alarmed when first a car and then a lumbering lorry stormed by.

"How fast they went," she thought, "how soon they became little and were gone." She was used to vans and lorries delivering in the market, but they had moved slowly and often went backwards.

After a while the buildings of the town ran out and there were no more pavements. Gracie trotted along on grass and gravel and she kept as far from the road as she could. There were so many things her mother hadn't told her about travelling. She hadn't told her that towns were so far apart. She hadn't told her that there were vast spaces with no buildings, no people and no smells of food. The size of nothingness was confusing to a dog who had never been outside a market before.

There were villages now and then, clean-smelling places where the houses didn't join up. There were shops and pubs, but they didn't have markets where you could hide on the dark side and meet other dogs like ... well, like Taters. There were no thrown-away scraps of food, and she was hungry. Tidy dogs barked at her from tidy gardens full of flowers that stuck out of the ground. Strange, thought Gracie, who knew about flowers. They came in bunches or in pots in the market, and you could move them about.

Gracie stopped when she could go no further because her legs ached, her paws were sore and she was hungrier than she had ever been. She crept into a dry ditch and slept soundly all through the night.

She moved on more slowly the next day because her legs felt stiff and the hunger was like a pain. But she was feeling cheerful because she sensed there was a town ahead. Then the sun came up and she came across a milkman's float. The milkman was gossiping in a doorway so Gracie helped herself to a large cut loaf which she took behind a hedge. She tore off the wrapping and gobbled it up several slices at a time.

The new town was nothing like the higgledy-piggledy town she had left. Everything in it seemed new and clean. Gracie wandered round looking for the sort of place where she could make herself a temporary home. She came to a large square where the ground was paved with coloured stones and there were trees growing in little cages. Bunches of people had gathered up one end of the square and were making a lot of noise. Gracie was puzzled by it all.

"I'm looking for the market," she said to a cat who was stalking a sparrow through a neat flower bed.

"You've found it then, haven't you?" said the cat crossly. "And I've lost that sparrow thanks to you."

"But there aren't any stalls," said Gracie.

"In there," said the cat pointing to a brick wall. "Go and see for yourself."

Gracie saw for herself and she didn't like it.

"Market indeed!" she sniffed, "It's more like a set of lock-up shops!" There was no way a dog could sneak in the backs of the stalls, under loose canvas. There was no interesting rubbish about and no dark side where a wandering stray could find shelter.

Gracie came out again, feeling cheated. The cat was still there. "It's not the sort of market I'm used to," Gracie said. "Where do you live?"

"In the theatre," said the cat, rather grandly.

"Oh, I see," said Gracie, scratching thoughtfully

and wondering if a theatre was another sort of market. "Could I stay there for a few days?"

"In a theatre? A dog?"

"Why not?" said Gracie indignantly. "What's so special about you?"

The cat sighed and swished his tail and then decided to be kind to this scruffy young pup who knew nothing about the world. "A theatre is a large building," he explained slowly. "People, called actors, go on a stage and ... act plays, and sing and dance sometimes. And lots of other people come and sit in velvet seats and watch them."

"They do? How funny. And that's your home, and those people look after you?"

"Certainly not. I am the Theatre Cat. You could say *I* look after *them*. It's a very responsible job, keeping the mice down in a theatre. I get well paid and the stage door keeper buys my food and ..." he clicked his claws fussily, "and anything else I might require." Gracie stared at him in amazement. If a cat could have a job ...

"Must be off now. Lots to do, you know. There's some street theatre going on over there, where the crowds are ... go and have a look." The cat stalked off importantly and Gracie just stared after him in admiration. The cat had a job. The cat was Someone. He got fed and housed and he didn't have to fight, he didn't have to belong to someone. He was his own sort of animal. Suddenly Gracie's head was full of dreams, and she knew why she had left Carter's Market. But she didn't know how to go about finding a job.

Gracie slunk through the forest of feet of the people who had gathered to enjoy the street theatre. She thought the people doing it were very peculiar, jiggling and shouting and laughing and singing. But they were having fun and she could feel the fun and it was good.

She lay under a bench chewing up a carton that had once held something sticky and sweet. She watched two people with noses like tomatoes falling down a lot and listened to someone making funny noises with spoons.

Then she stiffened. She sat up and banged her head on the bench. There was a dog – a dog standing up on its back legs and going round in circles, and then jumping through hoops. So they did have theatre dogs! The people watched and clapped and then the dog picked up a hat by the brim and went round the crowd. People were putting money in the hat and the dog was wagging its tail.

"I can do that!" Gracie said excitedly to herself, and without stopping to think that it might be difficult, she rushed into the actors' space. At first the audience thought that Gracie was part of the act – the joky dog who couldn't get anything right. But when she had fallen over a few times and tripped up a man with a drum, the actors started shouting at her.

"Get off! Go away, you're spoiling our act!" And then the audience started to boo. They sounded so unfriendly that Gracie stopped.

"I'll take the hat round instead," she said, and seized it in her mouth. Coins bounced out and rolled away. Someone shouted,

"Stop that thieving flea-bag! Catch it!" Gracie dropped the hat and fled through the crowd, with the actors' dog chasing after her.

Gracie was nimble. She soon escaped from the dog and hid under a concrete bench. A little old man and a little old lady were sitting on the bench, their feet swinging off the ground.

"There's a dog under there," said the little old lady, and her face appeared upside down peering at Gracie.

"Poor little thing, she's as thin as a piece of string." The little old man's upside-down face appeared.

"So she is," he said. "She looks scared to death. Someone must have frightened her."

They gave Gracie some jelly babies and some stale peanuts. She came out and sat in front of them. In a little while she realised, by the tone of their voices, that they were planning to take her home with them.

"Well, why not!' Gracie thought miserably. She had failed in her first effort to get a job and the acting people had been horrid to her. She had nowhere to go and nothing to eat ... and it was starting to rain ...

Chapter 3

The little old people were very kind. The first thing they did was to give her a nice meal out of a bowl and lots of milk. They gave her a bath and they showed her things that they seemed to think she would like – a basket with a blanket in it, a collar and lead, a ball and a squeaky pink toy shaped like a bone. They all smelled of another dog, but Gracie couldn't find one in the little flat.

Though she slept soundly in the other dog's bed and she ate greedily out of the other dog's bowl, she couldn't bring herself to play with the dreadful squeaky thing.

"Funny," said the old people. "Rover loved to play with it." Then they looked at each other a little sadly, remembering how much they missed old Rover. Gracie soon came to know that Rover had been a very old dog who had been happy to live at the old people's pace. But it didn't suit Gracie. The door was always kept tightly closed but in the middle of the morning, the couple slowly put on their coats, and they put Rover's collar and lead on Gracie, and they walked along together to the little corner shop. Then they came home again, and Gracie hid her head in the woman's skirt because she was so ashamed of being on a lead. What if Taters ever got to hear of it?

"Funny," said the old people, "Rover used to enjoy his little walk." They worried because Gracie was not happy with them. And Gracie worried because she could never be like Rover for them and she knew that she would have to leave soon. When the meals-on-wheels lady left the door open one day, Gracie slipped through it.

"Ah well," said the old people when they realised she had gone, "she was a stray and strays are like tramps. They like to keep moving."

Gracie moved on all day. It was getting dark when she saw a friendly orange glow in the sky and knew she was coming to a very big town. She felt smaller and smaller as she wandered the streets and the buildings seemed to grow taller and taller. Gracie had never seen so many bright lights, such huge shop windows and she felt uneasy. This was no place for a stray dog. She remembered her mother's warning.

"Wherever you go, be sure you have somewhere to run to, somewhere to hide *if you have to*." Gracie wasn't sure when a '*have to*' might happen. And there was nowhere, not so much as a shadow here. She saw a tramp rambling along the road, ferreting in the litter bins, and at once she felt better. A tramp would know where to go and sleep at night. She would follow him.

The tramp had a lot of pubs to call at before he finally wandered off into a dark alley and disappeared. Gracie just stood, sniffing the air and dribbling at the wonderful smells of cooking. They were better than the fish and chip van and the kebab vans that came to the market, a hundred times better. She saw a rat scrabbling on top of a dustbin lid. He stopped and sighed angrily and then he saw Gracie.

"What are you doing here?" he demanded, "this is my patch. This is my special bin and it's full of good things for me!"

"Well you can't get the lid off it, can you!" said Gracie cheekily.

The rat grunted.

"They don't usually put it on so tight," he said, scrabbling again. Gracie just waited.

"What is this place?" she asked.

"Papa's, Italian restaurant," said the rat. "It's my favourite, they throw away lots of cheese. There's an Indian Restaurant down there, or a nice steak bar if you're fussy. They've really squashed this lid down tight ... would you mind?" Gracie loosened the rubber edge of the lid with her teeth and then she pushed it off easily with her nose. The bin fell over. The rat plunged in greedily and, for a moment, only his excitedly twitching tail stuck out of the bin. Then his head appeared again.

"Pardon my manners," he said with a full mouth,

"but there's far too much for me in here tonight.
Dreadful waste – why don't you join me, be my
guest?"

"I'm going to," said Gracie, who'd only been put
off by the rat's strange behaviour.

"Leave the cheese for me, if you don't mind,"
said the rat, "and some of that crusty bread."

When Gracie had eaten so much rich food that she felt sick, she went and curled up in a doorway and slept deeply until there was a crash of glass followed by a strident bell ringing further up the alley. Gracie crawled behind a skip and peered out to see what was going on. The bell went on ringing, there were a few thuds and distant voices, and then the alley was suddenly ablaze with white lights and flashing blue lights. Two police cars stopped. Then to Gracie's amazement, a police van drew up and a policeman with a German shepherd dog jumped out of the back.

There were scrambling noises, some shouts and then a pleased voice calling,

"Okay. Victor's got him." A man was brought out between two of the policemen and bundled into a car. A little later, the dog appeared again, on a lead now, with a policeman who was patting him and saying,

"Well done, Victor. Good lad." The excitement over, the police cars went. It was quiet again. But Gracie couldn't go back to sleep. She tried to remember everything Taters had told her about policemen. Keep well away from them, he had said, they don't like us dogs and if there's any trouble they get us rounded up. But this policeman had liked the German shepherd well enough. He had been pleased with it. What had it done? Was it something she might be able to do too?

Gracie was up at dawn. She had a fishy meal from another dustbin and then wandered the streets again. She walked down a street that seemed to be edged with tall glass buildings. They were very slow to get up in this place, Gracie thought. The blind buildings stood in silence. No windows were thrown open, no people came out. No milk was delivered. Its eeriness was a solid thing. Later the traffic started and a few people came and unlocked the buildings from the outside. Some of them glanced at Gracie.

"Stray dog," said one. "Better report it."

Gracie understood their tone and she moved on quickly. Within an hour, the streets were full of traffic and the pavements full of people. Gracie had to scuttle about to avoid the feet. They came from everywhere, off buses, out of cars, they even came up from underground, like moles. Gracie was frightened, she wanted to get out of the crowd. Her instinct told her to go east where it would be safer. But east was the other side of the main road, now whizzing with traffic. Gracie began to panic. Her mother had warned her about traffic and now she knew why. When it was big like this it smelt of danger. She watched the people to see if they would try and cross a road this big and this terrifying. They did, and it was all so peculiar that Gracie had to sit and think about it. First they all got into a huddle on the pavement next to some lights on sticks. Then the lights changed and all the traffic stopped. When the traffic stopped there was a black and white striped path and they all hurried across it. Then the lights changed again and she could no longer see the path as the traffic flowed down the road again.

"Magic," breathed Gracie. The sort of magic Taters had talked about, black cats and witches and magic carpets. She watched the magic happen over and over again until she was sure that it always worked, and then she joined the huddle of people and was across the road and running along the other side.

She had been right to cross the road. The buildings were getting smaller. There were spaces in between, where weeds pushed through crumbling bricks, and there was a new smell in the air. It was less fumy, it was slightly dank ... A walled path tottered down a steep hill, and at the end of it there was a glint of water. Gracie trotted down it and suddenly she felt happy and free. The friendly path led her away from the noise of the city. She could breathe easily again, feel her half-grown size again.

She wasn't a slinking, skinny bit of a pup, in awe of big shops and pompous rats. She was Gracie, her mother's daughter, who was going to work out her own life. She was Tater's friend, who'd never be pushed about again, or put on a lead.

Chapter 4

The river was murky and had bits floating in it. Gracie had a long drink. She shook herself, sat in the sun having a thoughtful scratch and then followed the path that followed the river. Everything was new and interesting though not always nice. There was a poky bank of reeds, where ducks hid. When she put a paw into it, it sank and she drew back quickly and the ducks quacked and flapped in the water. Then there was an inlet full of murky brown bubbles and little streams, coming from a factory, that made puddles of oily colours. A grassy stretch led to a sandy bay, and then into another one where black plastic sacks spewed out mounds of rubble and metal and stringy paper. There was a bridge, and after the bridge, the path opened out into a timber yard where there were piles of planks and a musky smell of autumn in the air.

There was a dark blue van, too, parked near the river. In the van, behind a grating, there was a large and wolfy-looking German Shepherd. He growled menacingly when Gracie got close.

"Don't do that," said Gracie, going up to the little sideways opening window in the van. "You can't get out of there so don't think you can frighten me!"

"Get away. I'm on duty."

"I don't care what you're on. I saw you last night, didn't I? By the restaurant place. You were with a policeman."

"Of course I was with a policeman, I'm a police dog. Victor. Maybe you've heard of me. I've caught quite a lot of villains, had my picture in the papers ..."

"Oh," said Gracie in wonder, "so that's what you were doing last night! What else do you do?"

"I spend a lot of time just waiting," said Victor with feeling. "I saved someone from drowning in this river once. And I find things, people ..."

"How?"

"I use my nose. Sometimes they give you someone's smelly sock or something ... and you have to go and find the rest of him. It's quite difficult. Some dogs are specially trained to sniff out bombs and drugs ... some dogs patrol – I can do that. I went to a pop festival once." He stopped and waited for Gracie to be impressed. Gracie didn't know what a pop festival might be. She yawned, trying to hide her excitement. A police dog! Now that was something she could be. Something useful and important.

"I wouldn't mind going to a pop festival," Gracie said casually. "How do I go about being a police dog?"

"You?" Victor was really surprised. "You wouldn't go about it at all!"

"Why not?"

"Well ..." Victor considered her, "you're not a German shepherd or a labrador or a doberman for a start. You're a bit of a muddle ..."

"So what? I'm still a dog."

"And you're hardly fit and strong. I mean ... you're as skinny as a rat and you keep scratching."

"So I'll stop scratching. I'll get fat."

"That wouldn't be enough," said Victor. "We're all trained and ... er ... brave ..."

"Oh, brave are you?" said Gracie scathingly. "Hunky! Well, if being brave is enough I'll show you. I'll show you how tough and brave you get growing up in Carter's Market!" She looked around for something brave to do.

There was something. At first, she thought it was a log floating in the river. But it had arms. It nearly stood up and then went under the water. "A man!" thought Gracie excitedly.

"A man, struggling, drowning!" Without a thought for her own safety she hurled herself into the river to go to his rescue.

Swimming was easy. She just kept on running and there she was, in the water, dog-paddling towards the drowning man. She had to open her mouth very wide to grip his arm. Her teeth sank into something gungy. There was a scuffle, a lot of splashing and suddenly the man was standing up in the water, towering above her, and not drowning at all. He was angry. He was shouting, and Gracie was paddling away fast, with a mouthful of black sponge rubber.

Once on the bank she kept running. She heard a door slam and knew that Victor was coming after her. He was surprised to find how fast Gracie could run, but he cornered her under a thick hedge.

"Did you see?" Gracie puffed. "Did you see me being brave?"

"Being stupid!" said Victor crossly.

"But I nearly saved a man ..."

"You bit a policeman. You tore his wet suit. That was my boss, you dummy!"

"He didn't look like a policeman," said Gracie. "Why was he floating upside down in the river? Policemen usually stand up, on dry land."

"He was looking for some stolen silver. Now he's wet and cold and in a very bad mood. I'm supposed to catch you and take you back. But I'll let you go if you promise to keep off my patch, right?"

"Right, I'll go. I don't want to be a police dog any more. Well, not today, anyway. But I will get a job. And I'll do it really well, see if I don't!"

"Move!" said Victor. "Fast!" He watched her go. He wished her well, but he laughed to himself as he trotted back to his angry policeman – laughed to think that there was any job that a scrappy market mongrel like Gracie could do.

Gracie followed the tow-path until it stopped being a tow-path and became a river bank, with tall waving grasses, and meadows that stretched away for ever and ever. The buildings had got smaller and shrunk away without her noticing them going. The chemical smells had turned into sweet country air and the mechanical noises had stopped, so that she could hear the wind riffling in the trees and the river gurgling and giggling. Sometimes it raced itself across pebbles and sometimes it slid slowly into deep, dark pools. Gracie lay down to rest and think about it all. Being a city dog, she was nervous at first. Nervous of the stillness that was only broken by the whispering, humming sounds of nature going about its business. But then she felt calm, and then she felt very secure and then she was asleep.

She woke to her first country dawn. It was cold and dewy. All the creatures, down to the smallest ants, were busy and knew exactly what they were doing. The water rats made patterns in the river, rabbits lolloped through the grass and birds made dainty loops in the sky. Gracie sat and scratched. She was cold and hungry and she had no part in their dawn.

She thought about Taters, he'd be up and scrapping in the market ... and Victor, chasing baddies and sitting proudly in his special van ... and the little old people in their house, and the dancing dog and the city rat, coiled in spaghetti. And here *she* was, without any sort of purpose.

Time to move on again.

Chapter 5

There was a farm in the distance, tucked cosily into the curves of a hill. As Gracie approached it, she layered the air with her nose. She could smell crusty bread and fresh milk. There was a warm smell of cows and a sharp smell of pigs. She hurried along the farm track. An old sheepdog lay by the gate.

"Where do you think you're going?" he snarled tiredly.

"I'm looking for a job," said Gracie. "Do they have jobs for dogs on farms?"

"Certainly," said the sheepdog, looking at her curiously. "Have you had much working experience?"

"Some," said Gracie carelessly. "I worked with a theatre group ... for a little while. And I've done some police work."

"Really?" The old dog looked so surprised that Gracie hung her head.

"Well ... almost really ..." she said. "Well ... not really really at all ... I mean ... I used to live in a market and I want to work, and I've tried, but no one seems to want me."

"Come along," said the sheepdog kindly. "I'll show you around. Don't upset the chickens."

Gracie tiptoed carefully through the yard that was speckled with chickens. She noted their fluffy feathers and their wobbly combs and their spiky toes. She would remember, if she ever saw Taters again, to tell him that chickens didn't always come in boxes with chips.

"You look hungry, little market-pup," said the sheepdog. "Let's find you something to eat." They went round the farmyard, sniffing at food smells that were new to Gracie. She was hungry enough to eat the cabbage stalks that had been hung up for the chickens.

"Tut-tut-tut!" The old dog was most particular. He wouldn't let her eat the pig swill or the cattle cake or the chicken feed. "Greedy city habits!" he said, and showed her where his own biscuits were kept and the spare milk was stored.

"What sort of work can I do here?" Gracie said eagerly when she had eaten all she could. The sheepdog stared out over the hills pretending to think of something the scruffy little dog could do.

"Well? What do you do?" she asked impatiently.

"Nothing now, I'm old, I've retired."

"Oh. What did you do when you did do something then?"

"I'm a sheepdog. Sheepdogs round up sheep.

See that big flock of sheep up there on the hill? In my young day, I could gather them all up, take them twice round the hill and have them penned in a field south of Bogsdown before I'd had my breakfast."

"I can do that," said Gracie and she set off to go to work.

"No! Stop!" The sheepdog tried to catch up with her and failed. "Don't ... you have to know about sheep! You have to learn to work with a shepherd. Wait! Come back!"

Gracie could no longer hear him, and she wouldn't have stopped if she had. Not when there was work to do. She met a long, ambling string of cows coming along the road. A boy and a dog were chivvying them along.

"I'll help you!" said Gracie and she ran up and down the line of cows, barking at them to hurry up. Some of the cows ignored her and went on chewing grass and some of them made little kicking jumps and grunted.

"That's it, keep going!" Gracie yapped. "I'm a cow dog. Do as I say! Yap! Yap! Yip!"

The boy and the dog didn't seem very grateful. The boy glared and the dog growled but neither bothered Gracie. "Okay," she said, "you've brought the cows in. I'll get the sheep." She bounded away up the hill.

The sheep, who had looked like little wads of dirty cotton wool from the farm, turned out to be much bigger than Gracie when she got among them. For a few seconds she wondered if they might be fierce, if it would be better to leave them where they were, and find something smaller to round up ... like mice. But no! She was a farm dog now and she had to face the challenge.

She tried running round them, barking. Some of them looked up and some of them didn't bother, they just went on grazing.

"Please be rounded up," begged Gracie. "It's so important for my career."

The sheep weren't interested in Gracie's career, but they did get fed up with her and one of them started to move away. The others started to follow. Gracie rushed round them even faster and barked as loudly as she could. A lot of them were herded together now and going down the hill towards the farm. A lot of them scattered over the hill and shrugged their woolly shoulders.

"All right, I'll come back for you," Gracie shouted over her shoulder. "I don't mind doing two trips."

The sheep were moving in a fleecy crowd. They went quite fast. Gracie chivvied and bullied them. Some of them broke away in disgust, and some dawdled behind so she had to leave them. She still had about forty sheep rushing towards the farm, and she thought that would be enough to impress the farmer on her first job.

It was great, exciting, being a proper working dog – being in control of the sheep and having a definite purpose.

"Keep together," she puffed as they started to meander. "Please, please, you must!"

There was a huge oak tree on the side of the hill but Gracie realised that too late. She panicked, she didn't know what to do. They were heading for it at high speed. Horror of horrors! They would charge into it and bonk their woolly heads and knock themselves senseless!

They didn't. They weren't stupid. Half of them veered off to the right and disappeared into another field. The other half veered to the left and kept on going so Gracie chased them, knowing she had only a tenth of the flock left in her charge. She chased them across a field of new corn, through the farmer's wife's vegetable patch, trailing bean poles and kicking lettuces out of the ground. They couldn't stop now and Gracie certainly couldn't stop them. They rushed headlong towards the farmyard, scattering chickens and ducks and cats, and crashing into milk churns that bounced and bled milk. Bales of straw flew in the air and floated down in a musty shower. Some of the sheep ended up in the farm kitchen, bleating in confusion.

Gracie stood uncertainly in the middle of the yard. Her tail wagged so strongly that her head waved in rhythm. Surely someone would come soon to say how clever she was, to say how lucky they were to have found such a tough and resourceful farm dog right there, on the farm.

They came. They came with pitchforks and sticks and brooms. One of them had got a gun and was bending it in two.

The sheepdog came too. He chased her out of the farmyard and round the chicken sheds.

"Run! Run!" he growled.

"But why? I brought the sheep in, didn't I? Well, some of them. I can go back for the rest. I *can* be a proper farm dog. Did you see what I did?"

"Idiot! Sheep don't come in. They get moved to new pastures, carefully! Look at the damage you've made them do. Look at the others – they're scattered all over the place."

"But you said ... I tried ..."

"Go before you get shot. Farmers can shoot dogs who worry sheep, you know."

"But I didn't worry them. They were quite happy ..."

A shot ricocheted across the henhouses. Gracie recognised danger when it came close. She was running again, moving on to new pastures. She hoped she would find them soon.

She jumped a wall and ran along a curly lane until she found a van parked outside a farm cottage. The back was open and the van was half full of trays of eggs. There was just enough room for her to slip past the trays and find a little corner where she could crouch and hide. Someone came, bringing more trays of eggs. The trays were pushed back, their edges making squeaky noises as they moved. Gracie was pushed even further into her hiding place, three eggs broke over her back and she tried to eat them.

Then the van made a coughing noise and started to move. It bumped and swayed and swerved until Gracie thought she was going to be sick. The van ride was worse than anything she remembered. There was no way out, and every corner tightened her prison.

It seemed to Gracie to be weeks later when the van stopped. The trays of eggs moved away from her. There was a space to move. There were voices. There was a smell that seemed familiar. Gracie dragged herself stiffly towards the doors of the van and peered out. Another dog's nose was rooting into the eggs, greedily. The dog's head came into view, and the eyes stared in astonishment.

"Gracie!" said the greedy dog. "What are you doing in a van with all these eggs?"

"Taters!" said Gracie weakly.

Chapter 6

In many ways Gracie was pleased to be back in the market among her old friends. Taters laughed heartily at her adventures, and she had to tell him over and over again about the policeman, and the sheep rushing all over the hills.

"And now you're back," he said comfortably, "and you'll give up this silly idea about getting a job won't you?"

"Maybe," said Gracie. She hadn't quite given up. She had decided that she didn't want to do any of the things she had seen other dogs doing, but she didn't want to stay a market tramp all her life either.

"You going to join my pack?" Taters asked hopefully. Gracie had seen the pack. Five lean and mangy dogs who did nothing but scrap among themselves.

"No thanks. I don't like fighting."

"I do." He looked round to see if there was a dog looking for a scrap, but there wasn't. "Tell me about the sheep again, Gracie," Taters said. "Then we'll go see if the chip van's burnt any more chips."

Gracie soon slipped back into the old market routine, and she slept a lot because it was mainly boring. One morning she ventured into the craft section. Dogs rarely went there because they didn't sell food, just baskets and leather things and pottery. She found that a new stallholder had arrived since she went away, a jolly, friendly man called Mac who was a woodcarver. He worked away at his carving when he was not selling things to customers and Gracie watched him for a long time. There was something different about Mac and it puzzled Gracie. He never looked at what he was doing at all. When he talked to people, he never looked quite at them either. He had a dog, a labrador called Sally, who Gracie could see lying under the stall.

Gracie waited for her to come out, but she didn't until Mac suddenly called out, "Hey Joe, keep an eye on my stall will you, while I go to the loo?"

"Okay Mac. Get me a kebab on the way back, will you?"

Mac and Sally came out from the stall. Gracie stared in amazement. She had a handle coming out of her back and straps round her body. Mac held the handle as if he was going for a walk with a push-along toy. Gracie was so intrigued that she followed them all the way to the loo and back past the kebab van. They stopped and talked to Joe and then Mac went back to his stall, took the handle off Sally, and she lay down again. Gracie edged her way round to the stall.

"You're a nosy pup, aren't you?" said Sally, amused. "You've been staring at me for ages. You followed us through the market."

"Sorry," said Gracie, "but I've never seen a dog like you. You've got a handle on your back."

Sally smiled gently. "I'm a guide dog," she explained. "Mac is blind, you see."

"No, I don't see," admitted Gracie. "Is there something wrong with you?"

"No, no, dear. Mac is blind. He can't see. So I guide him."

Gracie stared, not quite believing what she had said.

"Can't see? Can't see at all?"

Mac called to Sally then and Gracie wandered off round the market thinking about them. It was most confusing. What did a guide dog do? She had seen Mac and Sally going through the market just like anyone else. Sally wasn't doing anything, she was just there. Of course Mac could see, he would bump into things if he couldn't. He wouldn't know where anything was. Gracie squeezed her own eyes tightly shut, then she took a few hesitant steps, and then a few more ... She bumped into a pram, knocked over a pile of flowerpots and then tripped someone up who shouted some extremely rude words, the sort that Taters sometimes used.

She opened her eyes and ran for cover. Then she thought she really ought to warn Sally about Mac.

She was lying under the stall again with her nose sticking out.

"Oh it's you again is it?" she asked.

"Sally, I've tried it. Going round the market without seeing. It's very dangerous. You bump into things. You mustn't let Mac do it!"

"Oh Gracie, you funny little worried thing! Mac's perfectly all right. He's got me. I'm his eyes, I see *for* him. That's what being a guide dog's all about!"

"You can't see for someone else. That doesn't make sense," Gracie said rather crossly because she thought Sally was making fun of her.

"Well I do. I've been doing it for ... oh, about eight years now. And Mac's never bumped into anything when he's been with me. We've been lost a few times in strange places, and I once took him to the Ladies instead of the Gents."

"Strange places?" Gracie said suspiciously. "You couldn't go to a big city. I've been to a big city. You have to cross terrifying roads in a city. You couldn't do that but I did it!"

"Clever old you!" said Sally. "You've travelled a lot for a youngster, haven't you?"

"Yes. Yes I have. I think I went to London. That's huge, isn't it?"

"It certainly is. We go there quite often. How did you get there?"

"Walked, of course. How do you get there?"

"We get a train to Waterloo, and if Mac says 'taxi' we just go across to the taxi queue and wait. And if he says 'bus' we have to go down some stairs, and then some more stairs and find the right bus stop, and then we get on a bus and get off it again and ..."

"Ah yes," said Gracie, "that's one way of doing it." Privately she thought that Sally was an even bigger liar than Taters. She decided to follow them when they went home that night.

It was Saturday night, the most muddly night of the week. Some stallholders were just packing up for the weekend, some were removing their stalls for a Sunday Market somewhere else. When Mac and Sally had closed their stall, there were people everywhere, piling crates and boxes, taking down lights, backing vans. Gracie followed them closely. In the few minutes it took them to work their way through the obstacle course of a closing market, she realised that Sally was a very special dog.

Mac strode out confidently, and it was only because Gracie was watching very carefully that she knew that it was Sally who saw the boxes in his path and led him round them. It was Sally who saw that an alleyway was blocked by a van, and stopped and turned to find another way round. It was Sally who saw a wire of light bulbs being lowered between two stalls, sat and obstinately waited. Sally who could have easily walked underneath the wire and didn't because it would have caught Mac round the neck. Gracie went back to the dark side of the market and lay down in a corner.

"Gracie? You all right?" Taters sounded anxious. Gracie didn't answer. "Some dog had a go at you? Gracie? Just tell me which one and I'll knock the brute from here to Tesco's. He'll never show his face in Carter's Market again. Some dog's going to wish it was never born. Trust me, Gracie!"

"Get lost, Taters!" she said tiredly. "I've met a dog today that makes you look like a bald two-legged rat."

"Oh you have, have you! That's great news, that is! I always thought, well, you and me ... So I was wrong. I suppose he's bigger than me, tougher ... maybe a good-looker. Well that's fine, you deserve it Gracie, you're a winner, that's for sure. Cheers." He went, and Gracie dreamed the sort of dreams that Taters, dear friend that he was, would never begin to dream.

Chapter 7

"Gracie, why do you follow us everywhere?" Sally asked the following Wednesday.

"Follow you? Do I?" said Gracie innocently. Sally just gave her a level stare. "I didn't think you'd noticed, you don't seem to," said Gracie, embarrassed.

"I have to concentrate all the time I'm working."

"I know, I've seen you. I've watched you crossing roads, even busy roads where there aren't any zebra crossings. I've seen you go into shops where other dogs can't go. I think you're just brilliant."

"Oh, thank you," said Sally. "It's just my job, really."

"Just your job," said Gracie thoughtfully, and then she told Sally about the jobs she had tried to get. Sally laughed as much as Taters had done about her adventures.

"Oh Gracie, you're a character!" she said, "Now you're back here and you've given up looking for work!"

"No," said Gracie very seriously. "Now I know exactly what I want to do. I want to be a guide dog, like you."

"You what?" Sally was about to laugh again, but she stopped herself when she realised how earnest

Gracie was. "Well ... you can't just be a guide dog like that ... I'm sorry but ..."

"Not 'just-like-that'," said Gracie indignantly. "I know I'd have to learn a few things first. But I could and I would. You could teach me."

Sally sighed deeply. "I'll have to think about it," she said, because she just didn't know how to tell Gracie that she couldn't ever be a guide dog. It wasn't possible.

"Well?" said Gracie after a little time had gone by.

"Guide dogs don't just *happen*. I was born to be a guide dog."

"I was born too!"

"I know but ... the people who train guide dogs, the Guide Dogs for the Blind Association, they choose them as puppies, they know who their mothers and fathers and grandparents are and what they're like ... and if they have the right sort of character ..."

"My mother was as good as your mother!"

"Yes, yes, but that's not the point. The Association don't know that. And guide-dog puppies are specially brought up in homes with children and cats, and they are taught to be obedient ... and then they go to a special school ..."

"Tell me where the school is, I'll go there."

"You can't. It costs lots of money! Four schools and a Brownie pack saved silver paper for years to pay for my training ..."

"Silver paper? Anyone can save silver paper. You're just trying to make it sound difficult. Why? Are you scared I'll pinch your job? Are you?"

"Gracie, that's fighting talk. You've grown up to a tough market life. I'd like you to have my job. I'm getting on a bit, but forget it because it won't happen."

Gracie nodded her head as if she agreed. But the tough market background was the one thing that made her more determined than ever that she could prove Sally wrong for once.

The stallholders in the market nicknamed Gracie "Mac's Shadow".

"What are you talking about?" asked Mac mystified.

"You've got a shadow, Mac, one of the young strays who live on the dark side. She follows you and Sally wherever you go. I even saw her outside your house late one night."

At first Mac was annoyed that he was being followed and worried that Sally might be distracted. But then he wondered *why*, and thinking about a stray dog sitting outside his house at night bothered him.

"This Shadow," he said to Joe, "what's she like?"

"That's the one they call Gracie," said Joe. "Difficult to describe. She's sort of black with white bits ... maybe a bit of collie and a bit of labrador and

something else. She's thin like the rest of them, but she's no trouble. Not like some of them."

"Is she young?"

"Oh yes. She's only about three-quarters grown. She disappeared for a bit, we hoped she'd found herself a home ... but back she came."

Mac took Sally for a run in the park on his way to work each day. The next day, when he had taken Sally's harness off and she had run off busily, he listened very hard for Gracie.

"Gracie?" he said gently. "You're there, aren't you? Why do you follow us? Gracie?"

Gracie took a few steps towards him. Sally came back. "Mac wants to meet you, Gracie. He knows about you."

"Well I'm here," said Gracie.

"Idiot! He doesn't know *where* you are. Touch him." Gracie went right up to Mac and let her nose touch his hand. He let her smell it and then he started to stroke her head and scratch her ears.

"So you're Gracie," he said. "Let's have a good look at you." Gracie stood still as Mac's hands ran all over her. He felt her ribs, and tutted. He patted her shoulder and felt her legs. No one had ever looked at her like that before and Gracie was proud that he was so interested and cared what sort of a dog she was.

Mac told his wife Annie about Gracie that night.

"Following you? How strange. Is that safe? Doesn't she bother Sally?" she said.

"She doesn't get in the way," said Mac slowly. "She's been doing it for weeks and I didn't know."

"You've been feeding her!" Annie said accusingly, because she knew what a softie he was with animals.

"I haven't. Promise I haven't. She isn't a scrounging stray, she's not like that. Look out of the window Annie and see if she's there."

Annie went to the window. There was silence for a minute.

"She is there, isn't she?" said Mac.

"Yes, she's there."

"What's she doing?"

"She's ... she's lying on the pavement with her nose pushed through the gate. Just ... looking. Waiting."

"I suppose we should do something about her," Mac said vaguely. "Get one of the animal rescue centres to come and take her away."

"I suppose so," Annie said. "I'll look up the number. You can ring them."

"Me?" said Mac uncomfortably. "I'm busy, couldn't you ring them?"

Annie looked out the window again. "No I couldn't, I'm going to get the supper." They both laughed. "Shall I let her in?" asked Annie.

"No!" said Mac firmly. "She's probably got fleas and worms and germs she might pass on to Sally. I bet she's hungry though. If we gave her something to eat it wouldn't be tempting her to stay. Not now when she's decided to stay anyway."

"It's starting to rain," said Annie. "She could have Sally's old basket in the shed ... just for tonight ..."

Every day Mac and Annie said "We'll do something about Gracie today" but the days grew into weeks and Gracie began to believe it would be forever. She slept in the shed, had good meals and went out every day following Sally and Mac to the market.

One morning Mac came out wearing a suit instead of his usual jeans and sweater.

"We're going to London today," Sally told Gracie.

"Oh good," said Gracie happily.

"Oh *Gracie!*" said Sally. "You can't come with us. When will you learn?"

"I need to learn about trains, don't I? When I'm a guide dog ..."

"Oh Gracie, grow up!" She didn't mean to sound cross, but she knew that Gracie was not going to be with them for much longer.

Chapter 8

Gracie followed Mac and Sally through unfamiliar roads to the station. She felt scared of the traffic but pretended to be brave like Sally. She had never been close to a train before and she didn't like the way the ground rumbled when one went by. Sally took no notice. She led Mac to a place in the ticket queue, and they moved up as the queue advanced. Gracie followed them to a booth where a man in a cap punched the ticket and then crashed a metal mesh gate in her face. Beyond it, Gracie could see Sally and Mac buying sweets and finding a seat to sit on. Then the horrid train came in and took them away.

Gracie felt she had been shut out, cut off. They hadn't said goodbye. She had no part in the pattern of their life.

Taters was pleased to see her back on the dark side of the market. "Given up your fancy friends, have you?" he said. "Or have they given up you?"

"Shut up, Taters."

"I did tell you, didn't I? Dogs like us weren't born to be slaves to people. We're free. Come and join my pack and forget about being a guide dog."

"I'll have to. I'm not clever enough to be a guide dog. I watched Sally today. I couldn't do the things she does."

"Course you *could*," said Taters indignantly, "but you *can't* because nobody will give you a chance." He sat and looked around, trying to find something that would cheer Gracie up. "Remember that silver paper you started collecting?"

"Yes!" said Gracie, brightening up.

"Dustmen took it."

"Oh. Thanks for telling me. There wasn't much, anyway."

They sat in silence side by side for a while. Gracie's head drooped miserably, but Taters was alert and planning.

"Tell you what," he said, suddenly seized with an idea.

"Go on ..."

"Supposing ... just supposing you did something terribly brave. Like saving Mac from ... from ... well, falling in a deep pit! Then you'd be a heroine, wouldn't you? Then everyone would say 'Hey! Did you see that? Did you see what brave Gracie did?' Then they'd make you a guide dog. Well, they'd have to!"

"Thanks, Taters," said Gracie. "Great idea, but it wouldn't work. For a start, Sally wouldn't let him fall in a pit. And for seconds, there aren't any deep pits around here."

"We could dig one," said Taters.

Gracie stared at him in horror. But he was so earnest about his idea that she had to laugh. It was Taters' way of doing things, it made sense to him. He was doing everything he could to try and help her.

"Oh Taters!" she said to herself, as she curled up at the back of the market. But when she slept, she dreamed his mad dreams about being a heroine and saving Mac, somehow.

The accident happened while she slept, and dreamed. It happened far away, and if she had been there, she wouldn't have been a heroine.

Gracie stayed in the market that night and went round to Mac's stall in the morning to wait for him to come with Sally and open it. He didn't come. One of Taters' brothers arrived in a hurry and tried to scrabble under Mac's stall.

"Help me, Gracie," he begged, "the pack's after me!"

"Get out of there!" snarled Gracie. "That's Mac's stall. I'm looking after it until he gets here."

"He's not coming. Hide me, Gracie. He had an accident, him and his dog. Haven't you heard?"

Gracie didn't wait to hear. She rushed round to the house. It was shut up. The way to her shed was barred. The curtains were drawn across the windows. Annie wasn't there. Gracie padded up and down the front, and up and down the back and no one came. No one came that night, though she waited and waited and got up, ready to greet every car that came down the road.

They came the next afternoon, in a car. There was a lot of fuss when it stopped. Annie was arguing with Mac about carrying a heavy bundle into the house. Mac carried it. The door was shut, the car roared away.

Gracie went on waiting and worrying. Where was Sally? Was it Sally in the bundle that Mac had carried in with such care? If it was, then why?

The front door opened and Mac came out. He had a long cane, painted white. He walked slowly, tapping the ground ahead of him, reaching out with it to find the gate. He opened it and called back to Annie,

"It's okay. I'll be back in an hour."

"Mac, let me come with you." She was standing on the step with her coat on, looking alarmed.

"No, don't," said Mac firmly. "Thanks Annie, but I can manage on my own."

Annie sighed miserably. Then, when Mac could not hear her footsteps, she crept down the path and through the gate. She saw Gracie padding along determinedly, several metres behind Mac. So they went, in an unlinked procession to the market. And they came back, keeping their silent distances.

When they were in the house again, Gracie went round the block to the entrance to the backyard and crept through the hole she had made in the fence.

It was a long time – it seemed to Gracie like her whole lifetime, before the back door was opened and Sally came out, slowly, painfully.

"Gracie?"

"Sally!"

The older dog limped down the path and squatted awkwardly. On and on it went. Gracie pretended to be looking for something in a flowerpot, but she was really glancing backwards at Sally. Her front leg was stiff, and a most peculiar shape. It had no hair on it. There were black criss-crosses down her leg and on her shoulder. Gracie was frightened because things she could not understand had happened to Sally.

Sally laid herself carefully on the path.

"Come here, Gracie," she said, "come." Gracie went towards her hesitantly and then stopped. "What's wrong?" Sally asked.

"Wrong?" said Gracie. "Nothing's wrong ..."

But everything was wrong. Gracie's animal instinct was saying to her ... that animal is sick and injured. Keep away. Leave it alone ... It is weak and cannot defend itself ... Keep away.

Taters would have kept away. He was wild. Mac and Annie would stay close to her with a special closeness because she was weakened. They were not wild. Gracie was just confused. Some of her wildness had gone since she'd known Mac and Sally, but not all of it.

"You're different. You smell horrible," Gracie said, taking another step towards Sally.

"I've been in hospital. The smell will go away. I'll get better. You don't have to be afraid, Gracie."

"You're not better now though. Sally? What happened? Why did you have an accident? Why?"

"Come and sit next to me. There, that's better. We went to London, remember? Mac had lunch with some friends, we were in a bus queue, on our way home ... it happened so quickly ..." Sally faltered and closed her eyes.

"What happened so quickly? What did?"

"It was raining, a van skidded, there was a dreadful squealing noise ... it came at us sideways ... and suddenly the people in the bus queue were scattered all over the pavement. They were screaming and bleeding ... then, I don't remember ... there were ambulances making whoooee noises, lights flashing ... I couldn't get up ..."

"Mac's all right," said Gracie. "Did you throw yourself in front of him and save him? Sally, did you?"

"I don't think so," said Sally with a little laugh. "We both fell over, he's got lots of bruises ... but at least the van didn't hit him." She looked ruefully at her puckered leg.

"They've put you together again, haven't they? How did that happen?"

"I'm not sure. They put my bones together and stitched me up while I was asleep. When I woke up, Mac was there and Annie had come. I must have gone to sleep for ages. Anyway, here I am! Mac went out today, didn't he? How did he get on?"

"He went to the market. It was awful. He had a long stick and he poked about with it, and went slowly, as if ... as if suddenly he couldn't see."

"He can't, you know that," said Sally gently.

"Of course I know that," Gracie said crossly, "but ... when he's with you, well, you can't tell he's blind. He's the same as someone who can see perfectly well!" Sally sighed deeply and shook her head.

"It's not your fault," Gracie said quickly. "You didn't want an accident to happen. I wanted to help him. I could have done you know."

"Gracie, you didn't ..."

"No. No, I just followed him. So did Annie, she was as scared as I was for him. There was just this once ..."

"Once? What?"

"When he got to the kerb on Market Street. There was a lot of traffic, and a car stopped because the driver saw him ... but there were other cars coming too ... I was so scared that I just ... well let him know I was there. I *had* to Sally ..."

"You didn't ... but I understand. Poor Gracie, you mean so well!"

"Meaning's not doing though, is it! He shouted at me and waved his stick. I was only trying to help." She sat back and scratched her ear. "It could have been my chance. My big chance of being a guide dog. I mean, if Mac knew what you know that I know ... if he knew *that,* well, then you know what I mean?"

"Er ... yes," said Sally, because in a roundabout way she did know what Gracie meant. She knew something else too. "Bob's coming this afternoon," she said casually.

"Bob?"

"He used to be my trainer at the dog school. He comes to see me every now and then to make sure I'm not getting into any bad habits, to see if I'm fit and ... well ... *capable.* That sort of thing."

"Oh," said Gracie, with all sorts of possibilities stirring in her mind.

"I'd be around if I were you," said Sally getting up painfully. "I must go in now, can't hang about, not like I used to ..."

Gracie took herself off for a long thinking-walk. She thought she knew what Sally had almost said. She came back and gave herself a good shake and licked her fur into place as neatly as she could. She was determined to be there when Bob came.

She saw his hurried walk up the path and his hesitant knock on the door. Mac opened it instantly.

"Bob! Good to see you!" Annie was right behind him. Their faces were like question marks. "You've seen the vet?"

"Yes," said Bob, "I've just come from his surgery. The good news is that Sally's going to be fine. She'll walk again on that leg. Of course, it's going to take time."

"And the bad news," said Mac slowly, "is that she's not going to be able to work any more. She can't go back to being a guide dog."

"I'm sorry Mac," said Bob, letting Mac take his arm as they went into the house.

Chapter 9

Bob stayed for tea with Mac and Annie and they talked about football and gardening and anything but dogs. Sally lay by the window. Every now and then she sat up and let her nose rest on the window sill. Bob looked at her curiously – he knew her better than anyone else except Mac.

"What is it, Sally?" he said. "Something outside bothering you?"

Mac and Annie turned to each other suddenly.

"Tell him," said Annie. "Tell Bob about Gracie."

"Is there a dog sitting outside the gate?" asked Mac.

"Yes. Whose is it?" Bob asked.

"No one's. It's Gracie, she's a stray from the market. She's attached herself to us. She's been following me round for weeks. You're not going to believe this, Bob, but I'm convinced she wants to be a guide dog."

"You're right," said Bob cheerfully. "I don't believe it. But go on."

"It's true," said Annie earnestly. "When Mac went to the market today she followed him. She kept out of his way, but she was so worried. When he came to a kerb she ran round in front of him as if she thought ... he might get run over. I could see the worry on her face!"

"You followed me!" said Mac accusingly.

"I'm sorry, Mac. But I was worried too. I didn't know you before you had Sally. I've never seen you without her. It was quite comic really, we went off in a little procession ... Gracie didn't know what to do when you got to the market, so she went ahead of you as if she was saying ... Look out! Mac's coming."

"I knew she was there," said Mac, "but I didn't know what she was doing. I shouted at her once to go away. Poor little Gracie, she was only showing me she was there."

Bob went outside and met Gracie. She was on her best behaviour. She wagged her tail and sat in front of him looking friendly and alert.

"So you're Gracie," said Bob. "Well ... I don't know what we're going to do with you, but you can't stay here." Gracie gave him a long look and then she took up her position by the gate again, looking at the house.

"Will she grow big enough to be a guide dog?" Annie asked anxiously.

"Well, probably. She'll fill out, needs feeding. I'll probably be able to find her a home."

"You do take dogs though, don't you, as old as that?" said Mac. "Don't you?"

"It has happened," said Bob, "just occasionally.

But we know a bit about their backgrounds, their temperament. With this one ... a stray ... she could be assessed but I wouldn't promise anything."

"I'm going to the paper shop," said Mac suddenly. "Just you watch!"

Gracie knew that the walk to the paper shop was going to be the most important walk of her life. Bob watched them carefully and he gave a little laugh of surprise.

"Extraordinary," he said. "She seems to understand ... she knows what she ought to do, but she doesn't know how to do it!" He opened the door of his car, Gracie looked from Annie to Mac. She looked back at the house, searching for Sally. Then she jumped in.

"I'll be in touch, Mac, about your new dog. I'm afraid there's a waiting list though. And I'll let you know what happens to this funny little creature too. Cheers!"

A lot of things happened to Gracie very quickly and some of them weren't very nice. She had a bath in something that smelt disgusting and stung. She was put on a table by a man in a white coat who stuck needles into her and cut her claws. When all that had happened, she was allowed into Bob's house and met his family. It wasn't a bit like living with the old people. She had to keep remembering all the things Sally had told her about her own puppy-walking days when she'd lived with a family. After her days in the market, it was difficult for her to stop herself from chasing the family cat, or eating anything that she found. She didn't like the children much because they teased her and dressed her up in silly clothes. They played with her, but when she ran off with one of their toys she got into trouble. She thought that a quick nip each would serve them right. That was the way younger dogs were treated in the market, and they learned their lesson. But Gracie knew Bob was watching her all the time and she controlled herself. He took her out for walks, he took her to his friends' houses, and once he took her to a noisy fairground at night.

"You're a good girl, Gracie," he said to her one night after she had been living in his house for six weeks. "Let's ring up Mac and tell him."

While Bob was talking to Mac about Sally's progress, he could hear Annie in the background saying, "Ask about Gracie, Mac. How's Gracie?"

Bob laughed. "She's just great," he said. "She's clean and confident and fit as a fiddle. I'm going to take her to the training centre tomorrow and let someone else assess her. It'll take a couple of weeks so keep your fingers crossed – no, don't bother. Gracie doesn't need luck. She's got the will to do anything!"

Gracie's will flagged several times over the months of training that she had to do after she had been accepted. She saw older dogs being taken away into the town wearing harness. The trainers wore blindfolds to pretend that they couldn't see.

"I know that!" she muttered. "They don't have to tell me!" She saw dogs going away proudly with their new owners, and she saw dogs who had worked very hard at their training going away to be pets because they just weren't good enough to be trusted as guide dogs.

The dogs in Gracie's class, the ones she played with when they had free time outside their kennels and runs, were mostly labradors and German shepherd dogs. They were suspicious of Gracie because she was different. She looked different, and the stories she told about her life and adventures were way out of their understanding.

"Okay, so I'm different," she said to them one day when they seemed to be ganging up on her, "but my best friend's a guide dog. I bet I know as much about being one as you do!"

She did her lessons, over and over again, in the safety of the centre, which was nothing like the real life she knew. She walked down the middle of the paths, keeping to the left of the trainer, just ahead, with her bottom level with his knees. She sat squarely and neatly at the kerbs. She knew when to sit and when to go, when to turn left and when to

turn right. She got used to the jokes, sudden obstacles in her way, other trainers suddenly backing cars onto the road. She learnt that she had to think for herself – and the person who would one day be with her, depending on her. She was taken into the busy town. She climbed stairs, went to shops. She went to a station and got on a train. She met cats and dogs and children and sudden noises and took no notice of them. So did the other dogs.

"What next?" she said to herself one day. "How long is this going to go on?"

She was fitted with a harness. She started to work wearing it. One day the trainers singled her out. It had been an ordinary sort of day. She'd been taken out, as the rest of her class had been, on a new obstacle course. A low arch had been put across the usual path. Gracie remembered seeing Sally taking Mac through the market. She remembered the string of lights way above Sally's head, remembered that Sally had known Mac would walk straight into them though she was below them. She stopped her trainer, sat, and then led him round a different way. All the other dogs led their trainer smack into the low arch.

Later on the same course, she had come to a fake kerb. She stopped, sat and waited for the traffic to pass until it was quiet. Then a car with its engine cut off had glided down the road. The trainer said

"Forward!" Gracie started to move, then

stopped. She sat, solidly. "Up! Help!" said the trainer. Gracie sat, and waited. She was taken back to her kennel. She thought she would get into trouble because she had been disobedient.

"But I had to," she thought, "that car wasn't making any noise. What else could I do? I had to disobey!"

The trainers were having supper that evening. They talked about the dogs and especially about Gracie.

"She knew about the arch," said one. "It usually takes several times to get that sort of thing through to them, but she saw it straight away."

"She refused to go when the silent car came. She knows she's in charge. I've never seen anything like it. That dog knows already that she's supposed to be working with someone who can't see!"

Bob said nothing, but he rang Mac again that night.

Another long month went by and still Gracie was not a guide dog. She began to wonder if she ever would be. She was tired of pretending that people were blind when she could be working with someone like Mac who really was.

Gracie knew vaguely what ought to happen because she'd been aware of it happening before. The centre's van arrived at the big house, which was a little way from the dogs' kennels. The new owners were taken into the house, and after a while their new dogs were taken away. Other young dogs came and took their places, the pattern went on.

Gracie knew that six blind people had come in. She knew they were in the house, and somehow she knew that Mac was among them. But he didn't come to see her.

For two days, she went on doing her training, going out for walks, playing with the other dogs. Mac knew that Gracie was there, waiting in her kennel. He hoped and prayed that she would pass her final test. He tried to picture her in his mind. She would be much bigger and fitter now, very well trained. There was a young girl on the same course that he was doing who was waiting for her first guide dog. Gracie would be right for her. He would feel so proud if Gracie made it. Sally would know too.

Mac remembered his first dog, a German shepherd called Max. It had been wonderful having Max, it had changed his whole life. They'd gone to college together and then Mac had been apprenticed to a master carver. He had started his own business. It had always been Mac and Max. They had climbed mountains in Scotland, they had been to concerts and sports meetings. After ten years, Max had to retire. He had gone to a good home but Mac had been heart-broken. He had even felt guilty starting all over again with Sally.

It was different this time. Sally could go on living with them because Annie was there to look after her when Mac went to work. He just hoped Sally wouldn't mind too much, seeing him go off with another dog each day.

The dogs in the kennels who sensed that their new owners had come were getting restless. Two days had gone by. Why didn't something happen? Had they failed, after all the work they had done? Didn't anyone want them?

The blind people in the centre were making friends, finding their way about the building. They went to lectures about looking after dogs, and those who hadn't had a guide dog before practised putting a harness on a model dog.

Then, one afternoon, they were asked to go to their rooms. The instructors had decided which people were best suited to which dogs. It was time for them to meet. Mac paced anxiously round his room. He checked twice to see that the new dog bed, the new lead and brush were all in the proper place and ready for his dog. He could hear doors opening and shutting, cheery voices, the sound of padded feet on the polished floors.

At last Mac's door opened.

"Here's your new dog, Mac," a woman's voice said. "Her name's Gracie. She's a mixture of collie and labrador, we think. She's black and white."

Gracie walked sedately up to Mac and put her head into his hands.

"I know what she's like," Mac said. "Thank you. Thank you very much." The door closed and they were alone. "You did it Gracie!" Mac said softly, "You *did* it!"

It was another three weeks before Mac and Gracie could go home. Gracie didn't mind because she was with Mac all the time. They went for walks in the town and in the country, they went on buses and trains, they went to shops and restaurants. Gracie didn't realise she was being watched by the instructors all the time to see she didn't make any mistakes. She had to prove that she could be trusted alone with Mac in the busy world away from the centre.

At last they were alone, on a busy station. Bob dropped them off and drove away.
"Home, Gracie," said Mac happily, and Gracie led him smoothly through the muddle of people and suitcases and into the station.

When they arrived Annie and Sally were there to meet them. Sally limped a little as she jumped out to greet them. She just stopped herself in time, and remembered that she had to sit quietly on the sidelines now. She was so proud of Gracie that she

didn't feel at all jealous. Gracie took no notice of her. She led Mac to the back of the car for him to put his suitcase in the boot, and then she led him to the door to get in. She was calm and completely collected until they had got into the house and Mac took her harness off. Then she went wild. She rushed up to Sally, she rushed up to Annie. She tore round the house giving little yelps of delight and then she gave herself a good shake and went to see if there was anything interesting happening in the kitchen, like food.

There was... Annie had made a special welcome home meal for Mac, and two special meals for Sally and Gracie, with bones for afters. They took them out in the garden.

Annie watched them through the window.

"She's grown into a beautiful dog, Mac. Are you sure it's the same scruffy little Gracie that used to sit outside the front gate? Wait till they see her in the market!"

·The market almost came to a standstill when they went back there the next morning. The stallholders cheered and shouted and gathered round to watch Gracie go by. Mac grinned and waved as Gracie went resolutely towards his stall, taking no notice of the welcoming clamour. When Mac had unpacked his stall and settled down to chat and carve, he took Gracie's harness off. She went and lay at the back of the stall, where she could push her nose out and see what was going on.

Taters was there. He was scratching nonchalantly.

"So you came back," he said. "Thought you might."

"Good to see you Taters. How's things?"

"Same as ever," said Taters. "You're a real guide dog now, aren't you? Where've you been all this time?"

"At school," said Gracie. "There was a lot I had to learn."

"They must have given you a lot to eat," said Taters enviously. "You're bigger than me now. You look pretty good too, sleek! Smart! Well I'm glad for you, you really wanted to be a guide dog didn't you? But you won't be my friend any more."

"Don't be daft Taters, I'll always be your friend. I can't run around with you like I used to, and I won't even notice you're there when I'm working but I'll be your friend all the same."

"Fine," said Taters, looking round to see if any of his pack were watching him. "Well, I can't sit about talking to a dog on a lead. I've got my position as pack leader to think of."

Mac dropped his chisel and Gracie went and found it for him. Taters watched her. He shook his head and walked arrogantly away.

Gracie watched him go. She wished she could

explain her new life to Taters but he would never understand. She was just a dog on a lead to him. "But you'll never know which end of the lead I'm on, Taters," she said to herself.